Whitney Wins

EVERYTHING

-A Tiny Ninja Book-

Written by Sasha Graham

Illustrated by Angelina Valieva

gatekeeper press™
Columbus, OH

Whitney Wins Everything: A Tiny Ninja Book

Published by Gatekeeper Press

2167 Stringtown Rd, Suite 109

Columbus, OH 43123-2989

www.GatekeeperPress.com

Library of Congress Control Number: 2021949760

ISBN (hardcover): 9781662908637

ISBN (paperback): 9781662908644

eISBN: 9781662908651

For the Marmots.
Thank you for reminding me of the magic that
comes from being part of a team.

Whitney was a passionate little girl who loved *a lot* of things. Crunchy dill pickles, glittery birthday parties, icky, sticky science experiments, and her snuggly kitten, Mac.

But there was one thing that Whitney loved more than anything else—more than pickles or parties or science or kittens . . . .

Whitney loved to win.

At home, she gobbled up the most mac and cheese, built the tallest towers, and beat her brothers to the bathroom to brush teeth.

At school, she was proud to be picked first for every team.

Everyone knew that Whitney ran faster, jumped higher, and scored more goals than anyone else. If Whitney was on your team, you were going to win.

Whitney's Tiny Ninja had always been there for her, cheering her on and helping her to be brave. The Tiny Ninja often reminded her that winning wasn't necessarily the most important thing every single time . . . but Whitney didn't always listen to her Tiny Ninja.

But Whitney knew better.
EVERYTHING was a competition.

One sunny day, Whitney saw Lily handing out the
most beautiful, sparkly envelopes she had ever seen.

"I'm not invited?" Whitney asked Olivia. "But . . . why?"

"Lily said they're going to have a lot of games at her party and that you would just win everything."

Whitney didn't know what to say, and her stomach hurt a little bit.

Whitney's day only got worse at her first
soccer practice that afternoon when her new
coach explained the rules.

"NO ONE KEEPS SCORE?! But . . .
how do you know who won?"

"Well, we play to be outside with our friends and to have
fun," said her coach. "So, if that's what happens, we win!"

Whitney had never heard anything more
ridiculous in her entire life.

Coach paired Whitney with Lily's cousin, Landon, to practice passing.

Landon was *terrible*.

"Is this your first time playing soccer?" Whitney asked carefully.

Landon laughed, "No, I'm just not very good."

"No offense, but then why do you play?" asked Whitney.

"Well, I like it, I guess. I mean, it's still fun," Landon replied.

Whitney was *very* confused.

That Saturday, Whitney played her heart out until Coach had her take a break.

"Weird," Whitney said to her Tiny Ninja who was sitting quietly beside her. "Landon keeps messing up but they're still cheering for him."

"Maybe that's *why* they're cheering for him."

"Because he's bad?"

"Because he's trying. Plus, look, he's having fun!"

Sure enough, Whitney watched as Landon completely missed the ball and toppled in a heap on the ground. But instead of getting mad, he just laughed, jumped up, and ran after the other players.

With just two minutes left in the game,
Coach finally put Whitney back in and
she was ready to win! She easily stole
the ball and sprinted for the goal.

Whitney felt strong and fast, and she
could hear people cheering her name.
She zeroed in on her target.

She pulled her leg
back, ready to fire, but
at the last second she
noticed her Tiny Ninja.

Whitney stopped. She could hear everyone on the sidelines hollering at her to shoot. But she *didn't*.

Instead, she took a deep breath and very gently passed the ball to Landon then watched in horror as it bounced off his shin guards.

"Landon!" Whitney screamed as loud as she could. "Kick. The. Ball. Into. The. Goal!"

So he did.

For one long second, nothing happened, then the game was over. Coach was telling her it was a dynamite pass, her dad said it was great that she trusted her teammate, and Landon's mom was squeezing her in a tight hug.

Landon worked his way over to Whitney, looking a little stunned.

"Did we win?" Landon asked.

Whitney held up her hand for a high-five. "Definitely."

"Um, Whitney?" Lily asked. "Do you think you might like to come to my birthday party later?"

"Oh, yes!" Whitney exclaimed. "And I'll definitely let you guys win when we play the games!"

Everyone laughed. Whitney didn't *really* understand what was so funny, but she laughed too.

As she walked to the car after the game, Whitney felt happy. Maybe even as happy as if she had scored that goal herself.

Whitney turned to her Tiny Ninja and whispered, "Tiny Ninja, how long will you stay?"

"Forever."

"Even when I'm a grown-up?"

"Especially when you're a grown-up."

"That's good," Whitney replied with a smile. "I have a feeling I'm going to need you."